A Fairyland
Ferry Adventure

Written by Kathleen Whitham
Illustrated by Mina Anguelova

Printed in the United States of America

ISBN 979-8-89114-221-3 (sc)
ISBN 979-8-89114-222-0 (hc)
ISBN 979-8-89114-223-7 (e)

Library of Congress Preassigned Control Number: 2025918398

2025.10.28

MainSpring Books
5901 W. Century Blvd
Suite 750
Los Angeles, CA, US, 90045

www.mainspringbooks.com

Dedicated to my eight grandchildren:
Carter, Jack, Lincoln, Cole, Graham, Amelia, Wells, and Olivia.

"I'm so excited to spend Father's Day weekend with our dads and the two of you at the beach," declared Olivia to her cousins, Cole and Lincoln.

"Yes, me too," responded Lincoln enthusiastically. "School's out for the summer, it's a beautiful day, and here we are on the ferry headed for the Outer Banks of North Carolina. We're so lucky!"

"We really are," Cole responded. "I can't wait to play in the sand and surf and find out what other adventures await us. We always have such fun together!"

The three cousins stood by the railing of the ferryboat as it was approaching the island, and they could distinguish the docks and other boats and houses and beaches coming into view more and more clearly, as seagulls and pelicans sailed by overhead. Suddenly, a big bump let them know they had arrived. "We'll get off the boat and wait for you at the end of the gangway," Olivia called out to the three dads who were busy gathering all the beach equipment. The three cousins each grabbed a suitcase and beach bag and hurried down the ramp.

When they reached the bottom, they quickly looked around to take in the sights, and there in the distance, they could make out another very small ferryboat shining in the sunlight but casting an additional eerie glow.

"Oh wow, do you see that?" asked Cole.

"Yes," answered Lincoln. "What can it be?"

"There's a stairway leading up to the entrance of the boat, but no one is getting on or off," observed Olivia.

"It actually looks a little spooky," said Cole. "And there's something written on the side of it."

"Let's take a look while our dads are gathering everything together," suggested Lincoln. They left their belongings on the dock and ran towards the mysterious boat.

"Look," said Olivia with excitement, "it says Fairyland Ferry in gleaming letters on the side."

FAIRYLAND FERRY

Suddenly they heard a booming voice: "Good afternoon, Fairyland adventurers. This is Captain Conte de Fée speaking. All Aboard for Fairyland! Hurry and climb the stairs and we'll be off on our Fairyland adventure. It may seem to be a long trip, but in outside-world time, it'll last less than a minute. No one will realize you're gone."

With this irresistible invitation, the three children bounded up the stairsteps and onto the boat, and off they went. Captain Conte de Fée explained what they could expect: "There will be a series of very small islands, each one representing the area or country where particular fairytales originated. You do need to be aware that many of these tales were modified or rewritten numerous times throughout their development. I think you'll enjoy seeing various characters that you've already met through storybooks, and you'll probably meet some new ones as well. Also, think about what each story teaches us. Let 's go--Allons-y!"

The tiny ferryboat chugged along the coast as the children looked at the land on the shore zipping by. "Look!" exclaimed Olivia. "I've been to France, and I see a French flag, blue, white and red, flying above the first little island."

"It seems like we're slowing down," observed Cole.

"Yes, we are slowing down but we're still moving," said Lincoln. "I don't think we'll stop."

"Hey," exclaimed Olivia. "I can see the Little Prince and Little Red Riding Hood over there."

"Right," Cole chimed in. "There's Little Red Riding Hood with her basket of goodies, her grandmother's house off in the distance, and a wolf hiding behind a bush."

"We all know that story, but what would you say its main lesson is?" asked Lincoln.

"Always be nice to your grandma, and don't trust wolves or anyone you don't know well," stated Cole.

"Complete the task you need to do and don't get distracted along the way," added Olivia.

"The little Prince" is one of my favorite stories," commented Lincoln.

"What's it about?" asked Olivia.

"It's about a little boy who loves a beautiful flower and becomes friends with a fox," replied Lincoln, "plus love and friendship and loyalty and fond memories. The fox, after becoming friends with the Little Prince, says he'll miss him when he's gone, but since the prince's hair is the color of the wheatfields, the fox will love the sound of the wind in the wheat and will always remember his friend."

"I want to read that book," said Cole. "Now I see two other island dwellers: Beauty and the Beast, a story about a beautiful princess and a prince who had been turned into a beast by an evil spell. Beauty, the princess, falls in love with him in spite of his beastly appearance, and the spell is broken by their true love. "

"I bet I know the moral and that tale," announced Olivia. "It's what's inside that counts. Your inner beauty, like being kind and loving, is more important than outer beauty."

"Look over there," Lincoln pointed ahead. "We're approaching another small island and I see a black, red, and gold flag overhead. It's the flag of Germany."

"What fairytale characters might be living on this island?" Olivia wondered.

"I know there are several Brothers Grimm characters around, and sometimes they can be pretty 'grim'—pardon the pun," Cole smiled.

"Look, I see Snow White and the seven dwarfs hanging out in the dwarfs' cottage, and I can hear the evil queen back in the castle asking her magic mirror who's the fairest of them all," observed Lincoln.

"Be careful, Snow White. The queen is very jealous and dangerous," Olivia warned. "What will happen if the mirror answers that Snow White is the most beautiful?"

"I guess we'll just have to read the story," Lincoln replied.

"What are some lessons we can learn from this?" asked Olivia.

"Well, don't get jealous, don't accept apples from evil queens, and someday your prince will come and everything will end well, so never give up," Cole, who was already familiar with this story, summed up. "Hey," he added. "I hear a little elf-type-guy laughing and repeating 'Rumpelstiltskin is my name.' What's the story behind that?"

Lincoln began to explain: "The story, Rumpelstiltskin, is about a poor man who tries to impress the king by telling him that his daughter can spin straw into gold. The greedy king responds by locking her in a straw-filled tower conveniently equipped with a spinning wheel and tells her to get to work spinning gold. A little elf-like man named Rumpelstiltskin appears in the tower and offers to 'help' her (for a price). You'll have to read the story to find out what happens."

"I bet I know some lessons to take away from this," Olivia commented. "Don't promise what you can't deliver, don't be greedy, and you don't need to try to impress others. Be happy with who you are."

"Up ahead in the distance, I see the British flag...red, white, and blue, like ours," Cole declared with enthusiasm. "And there's Goldilocks skipping along through the forest."

"There are a lot of threes in this story, as in many folktales," noted Lincoln. "Three bowls of porridge, three chairs, three beds, and three bears!"

"The lesson from this story must be, don't barge into strangers' homes and eat their food and break their chairs and sleep in their beds," Olivia chuckled.

"It might also be to seek that which is 'just right'—avoid too much or too little of anything," suggested Cole.

"Hey, guys, look over there," said Lincoln. "I see a pile of straw, a pile of sticks, and a sturdy-looking brick house with three little pigs hanging out. It's another three story."

"It looks as though the big bad wolf has already huffed and puffed and blown down the houses of straw and sticks," observed Cole.

"Here's the lesson," concluded Olivia. "Build things to last with sturdy materials and a solid foundation."

"I see a Danish flag on the next island," announced Olivia. "Red with a white cross."

"Hans Christian Anderson, who wrote many fairytales, came from Denmark," noted Cole. "Hey, what's that swimming beside our ferryboat?"

"It looks like a mermaid!" answered Lincoln. "Yes, it must be 'The Little Mermaid' by this author. I also see a little duck swimming in the water."

"Of course," said Olivia. "It's probably the 'Ugly Duckling,' which will end up becoming a beautiful swan. So, never make fun of others because, first, it's really mean, and also, you never know how things may change in the end."

"My favorite story is 'The Emperor's New Clothes'," Cole revealed.

"What's that about?" asked Olivia.

Cole explained: "There's this self-important emperor who hires two dishonest weavers to make him a beautiful suit. These weavers say they have special cloth that's invisible to anyone who's not so bright. They really have no cloth at all, but everyone pretends to see the new "suit," including the emperor himself, and they all rave over how beautiful it is. When the emperor "wears" it proudly for the first time in public, everyone oohs and ahs until a small child shouts out, 'Hey, the emperor is wearing nothing at all!'

"The lesson? Don't follow the crowd or be afraid to say what you think." Lincoln stated. "The little child is the only one who speaks the truth."

Olivia clapped her hands in excitement: "I see another island and there's a green, red, and white flag flying overhead. It must refer to Italy."

"Look, there's Pinocchio, and I also recognize Father Geppetto, the poor woodcarver who made Pinocchio, the puppet who dreamed of becoming a real boy, just like you and me, Cole," said Lincoln enthusiastically.

"And there's the Turquoise-haired fairy who helps Pinocchio achieve his goal," Cole pointed out. "Uh oh! His nose is looking a little long. He must have been lying recently."

"One of the morals of this story must be, tell the truth, don't lie," Olivia concluded.

"I also like the idea that dreams can come true, so keep your dreams alive," added Lincoln.

"Hey look—we're back in the USA! Here's an island with our red, white and blue stars and stripes," said Cole.

"Oh my, I see a super-big man with a huge blue ox over there," declared Olivia. "Who are they?"

"It must be Babe, the Blue Ox, and Paul Bunyan, a giant lumberjack and hero of tall tales. There are all kinds of legends surrounding those two," explained Lincoln.

"I see a lot of other animals in the forest. What's their significance?" asked Olivia.

"Many of them are part of Native American folklore tradition," replied Lincoln.

"At school in November, which is Native American Heritage month, we read a number of stories about animals," explained Cole. "One I really liked was about Raven, a 'trickster' type, causing Crow to lose his beautiful singing voice through flattery and deception. Another story I remember was about how the chipmunk got its stripes."

"I see a crow, an owl, an eagle. a bear, a coyote, a buffalo, a deer, and a turtle over there. What do they all represent?" wondered Olivia.

"Hey, there's a fun little quiz at the end of this book that relates to that," answered Cole. "Try it. It shows how much Native Americans are connected to the spiritual world and to nature."

"Who's that little girl skipping along carrying a small dog?" asked Olivia.

"I believe it's Dorothy with Toto from The Wizard of Oz. I see the Tin man, the Scarecrow, and the cowardly Lion, plus a bunch of little people running around," responded Lincoln.

"Yes, those are the Munchkins. I wonder what the moral of this story is," said Cole.

"Maybe there's no place like home. And to believe in yourself—you can do just about anything with heart, brains, and courage," Olivia recapped. "And magic shoes are always helpful."

"Look," observed Cole, "we're turning around. It looks like we're heading back, and we're traveling pretty fast."

"I can't wait to wish our dads a happy Father's Day and have a little cookout down on the beach. Maybe some hotdogs and marshmallows and S'mores," Lincoln smiled with anticipation.

"I loved our fairyland ferry adventure," declared Cole.

"It seems like we visited storylands from the northern hemisphere and Western Europe. It would be fun to do another voyage concentrating on folklore and fairytales from the southern hemisphere and the Far East." Lincoln suggested.

"For sure!" responded Olivia. "We'll definitely plan this other adventure for a later date. Today was so interesting and I learned a ton. I can't wait to go to the library to find these stories and read them."

"Hey, here we are!" announced Cole. The three of them got off the Fairyland Ferry after thanking Captain Conte de Fée with heartfelt gratitude. Righy away they spotted their dads waiting with suitcases and beach supplies beside their original dock. "Happy Father's Day! We love you!" they called out, running towards their three dads with arms outtretched.

Notes

Conte de Fée means fairy tale. Pronounced: conte (rhymes with don't) duh (say quickly) Fée (sounds like Faye, (last syllable is emphasized in French)

Allons-y, French for "Let's go." Pronounce "ah-lone-zee.

Le Petit Prince, by Antoine de Saint-Exupéry, was first published in 1943.

"Little Red Riding Hood" and "Sleeping Beauty" were part of a collection of fairy tales by Charles Perrault published in 1697.

The Brothers Grimm were collectors of fairy tales, including "Snow White" and "Rumpelstiltskin," published in 1812,

"The Three Bears," by Robert Southey, is an English fairytale originally published in 1837.

"The Three Little Pigs," by James Halliwell Phillips, was published in 1886.

Hans Christian Anderson (1805-1875) from Denmark, wrote many well-known fairytales, including "The Little Mermaid," "The Ugly Duckling," and "The Emperor's New Clothes."

The Adventures of Pinocchio was written in 1883 by Carlo Collodi.

Paul Bunyan and Babe the Blue Ox are folk heroes of American and Canadian folklore.

The Wonderful Wizard of Oz is a 1900 children's novel by Frank Baum.

Here's the Native American animal quiz:

what does each represent?

1._____Bear   a. renewal, masculinity, teacher, patience

2._____Coyote   b. gentleness, fertility, grace, femininity

3._____Deer   c. freedom, courage, connection to spiritual
                          world, messenger

4._____Elk   d. leadership, power, protection, strength

5._____Otter   e. longevity, wisdom, Mother Earth

6._____Butterfly   f. hardworking, determined, strong-willed

7._____Buffalo   g. intelligence, mischief, trickster animal

8._____Eagle   h. sacred animal, life, unity, strength,
                          stability

9._____Turtle   i. "river wolf," symbol of playfulness,
                          resilience, resourcefulness, community

10._____Beaver   j. transformation, grace, renewal, hope

Answers: 1d / 2g / 3b / 4a / 5i / 6j / 7h / 8c / 9e / 10f /

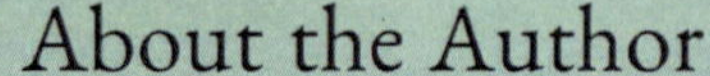

About the Author

Kathleen Whitham, who holds an AB degree from Indiana University and graduate degrees from the University of North Carolina, was a French and Spanish teacher for over forty years. She is presently the owner and pastry chef of a pie and pastry business in Hillsborough NC. However, she considers her role as the mother of five sons and the grandmother of eight as the role of greatest importance in her life. For the past several years, she has enjoyed writing books for her grandchildren, many with a holiday theme, and this has been the inspiration for the books she has published so far. She hopes that you and the children in your life enjoy this book as much as she enjoyed creating it.